OOPS! ACCIDENTAL INVENTIONS

SPRAY STRING

by Catherine C. Finan

Consultant: Beth Gambro
Reading Specialist, Yorkville, Illinois

BEARPORT
PUBLISHING

Minneapolis, Minnesota

Teaching Tips

Before Reading
- Look at the cover of the book. Discuss the picture and the title.
- Ask readers to brainstorm a list of what they already know about spray string. What can they expect to see in this book?
- Go on a picture walk, looking through the pictures to discuss vocabulary and make predictions about the text.

During Reading
- Read for purpose. Encourage readers to think about spray string as they are reading.
- Ask readers to look for the details of the book. What happened to take spray string from an accident to a favorite toy?
- If readers encounter an unknown word, ask them to look at the sounds in the word. Then, ask them to look at the rest of the page. Are there any clues to help them understand?

After Reading
- Encourage readers to pick a buddy and reread the book together.
- Ask readers to name two things that happened when spray string was being developed. Find the pages that tell about these things.
- Ask readers to write or draw something they learned about the creation of spray string.

Credits:
Cover and title page, © JStaley401/Shutterstock; 3, © Sonya Etchison/Dreamstime; 5, © sonya etchison/Shutterstock; 7, © GetYourPic/iStock and © martinedoucet/iStock; 9, © ronnachaipark/iStock; 11, © Michael P. D'Arco/Shutterstock; 12–13, © FabrikaSimf/Shutterstock and © New Africa/Shutterstock; 15, © Hola Images/Getty Images; 17, © GlowImages/Alamy; 19, © Africa Studio/Shutterstock; 20–21, © Comstock Images/Getty Images; 22TL, © Talaj/iStock; 22MR, © Flashpop/Getty Images; 22BL, © KsanderDN/Shutterstock; 23TL, © altmodern/iStock; 23TM, © FangXiaNuo/iStock; 23TR, © alacatr/iStock; 23BL, © Michael P. D'Arco/Shutterstock; 23BM, © ijeab/iStock; and 23BR, © scanrail/iStock.

Library of Congress Cataloging-in-Publication Data is available at www.loc.gov or upon request from the publisher.

ISBN: 979-8-88509-345-3 (hardcover)
ISBN: 979-8-88509-467-2 (paperback)
ISBN: 979-8-88509-582-2 (ebook)

Copyright © 2023 Bearport Publishing Company. All rights reserved. No part of this publication may be reproduced in whole or in part, stored in any retrieval system, or transmitted in any form or by any means, electronic, mechanical, photocopying, recording, or otherwise, without written permission from the publisher.

For more information, write to Bearport Publishing, 5357 Penn Avenue South, Minneapolis, MN 55419.

Contents

A Stringy Accident............. 4

Spray String Today 22

Glossary 23

Index 24

Read More 24

Learn More Online........................ 24

About the Author 24

A Stringy Accident

Wet, colorful pieces fly through the air.

Spray string is lots of fun.

How did this silly **invention** happen?

> Say invention like in-VEN-chuhn

5

The first spray string was made in 1972.

It happened by **accident**.

Oops!

> Say accident like
> AK-si-duhnt

7

Robert Cox and Leonard Fish made a new **plastic**.

They wanted to use it in **casts** for broken bones.

A cast

The plastic could spray from a can.

It came out **foamy** and sticky.

Then, it would turn hard.

11

12

Robert and Leonard wanted to find the best spray can.

They tried hundreds of them.

One sprayed the plastic very far!

This gave Robert and Leonard a new idea.

The plastic could be a fun string toy!

They changed it to be less sticky.

15

Then, they met with a **company** to sell the toy.

They sprayed their string everywhere!

17

At first, the company did not like spray string.

But later, they changed their minds.

They started selling it.

19

The new toy was a hit!

People still spray it for fun today.

And it is all thanks to a silly accident.

21

Spray String Today

Today, spray string comes in many colors.

Some people use spray string to celebrate.

The world's biggest spray string fight used more than 4,000 cans!

Glossary

accident something that is not planned

casts coverings that help broken bones heal

company a business that sells things

foamy with many bubbles

invention something new that people have made

plastic a human-made material that can be shaped into many things

Index

can 10, 13, 22
cast 8–9
colors 4, 22
Cox, Robert 8, 13–14
Fish, Leonard 8, 13–14
plastic 8, 10, 13–14

Read More

Berne, Emma Carlson. *Toys and Games (Past and Present).* Minneapolis: Bearport Publishing, 2023.

Waxman, Laura Hamilton. *Cool Kid Inventions (Lightning Bolt Books: Kids in Charge!).* Minneapolis: Lerner Publications, 2020.

Learn More Online

1. Go to **www.factsurfer.com** or scan the QR code below.
2. Enter **"Spray String"** into the search box.
3. Click on the cover of this book to see a list of websites.

About the Author

Catherine C. Finan is a writer living in northeast Pennsylvania. She made a spray string sculpture of her pet dog when she was eight years old.